happily evan after

dog tags

book five

Kat Baxter

Happily Evan After

Kat Baxter

Edited by: Emily Beierle-McKaskle

Copyeditor: Geeky Girl Author Services

Book cover: Cormar Covers

Cover image: Jane Ashley Converse Photography and Images

Cover model: Calvin Boling

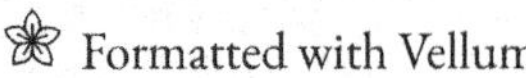

happily evan after

SHE'S SCARED TO FALL. He's ready to catch her.

MARLEY

It was one night.
No names. No strings.
Just the kind of reckless escape I never let myself have—until him.
Now he's standing in my clinic, smiling like he doesn't remember me.
Which is fine. Because Evan Cartwright is too young, too charming, and way too dangerous to my heart.

EVAN

I knew it was her the moment I saw her.
The woman I've been thinking about for months.
She acts like we've never met, and I let her.
Because now that I've found her, I'm not letting go.
Even if she's keeping one hell of a secret.
Even if she thinks I'm not ready.
I've never backed down from a challenge...
and I've never wanted anything more.

chapter **one**

MARLEY

Six months ago...

"There comes a time in every woman's life when she has to grab the bull by the dick."

I burst out laughing. "That is not how the saying goes." I stare at my closest friend as she stands behind the bar where she works, slinging drinks, making quips, and probably earning more in tips than I do as a veterinarian. Of course, it doesn't hurt that her family owns the bar. She has more bravado and confidence in her little toe than I have in my entire body. "How are we even friends?"

"Because, sugar tits, every super smart, neurospicy girl needs a crazy friend with no filter."

I shrug and smile at Lana. "I suppose that's true."

"Let's get back to the conversation we were having."

"What conversation? You were trying to ply me with liquor." I swirl my wine glass.

"Chardonnay is a lonely woman's drink."

I shrug again. "Goes with all the cat hair on my pants."

"Marley! You have something to celebrate! You are about to own your own veterinary practice. That's huge," Lana says. She leans forward, bracing her elbows on the heavily polished wood in front of her.

"I think it might be a little less impressive than this bar. It's swanky."

She lifts a shoulder, causing her shirt to fall off said shoulder, revealing the colorful tattoos that cover most of her right arm.

"Stop avoiding the conversation," she says.

I blow out a breath. "I'm fully aware that you think I need to get laid."

"I know you need to. If it's been as long as I'm thinking it has, then I'm pretty sure there might be cobwebs in your lady garden."

That makes me snicker. "You are mixing your metaphors again. And yes, it's been that long."

"Jason? Junior year?" she asks.

"Yes. He kept his socks on the whole time. It was weird."

"Pre-med students are weird." She tops off my Chardonnay. "Not that you vets are much different."

"Oh, I'd much rather deal with animals all day than people."

"Same. But a bar for dogs hasn't caught on," Lana says with a grin. She leans a little closer to me. "All I'm saying is that you could have your pick of some very attractive men who have been checking you out since you walked in."

I scoff. "As if. I've never had to pick because there hasn't ever been enough for a choice. Which is fine because I'm picky." Still, my curiosity niggles at the back of my brain. "But just because I'm nosy, who are we talking about, hypothetically?"

"Hypothetically, there's a total bro-man at one of the back tables. He's cute enough, but I'd be willing to bet he wears loafers ironically."

I snort-laugh. "I don't even know what that means." I don't even bother turning around to look. "Why don't you just tell me which one you think I should go home with?"

Lana's eyes flash. "That's the spirit, sugar tits." She leans forward over the bar as if to give me a hug, but instead she whispers in my ear. "At the far end of the bar, sitting by himself is a hot young thing who hasn't been able to take his eyes off of you."

Before I can ask what she means, a customer comes up to the bar and Lana excuses herself for a moment to get their drink, but not before waggling her eyebrows suggestively.

Hot young thing? What does that mean? This is a bar; whoever she's seen can't be that young.

I try to be casual as I turn my head to the right to see the end of the bar. Is she messing with me? Because the man at the end of the bar —currently talking to two women in skimpy dresses—is, hands-down, the most attractive human I've ever seen. Male or female. He's just beautiful, there's no other way to describe him.

His jawline is so chiseled, it must be the one that broke the proverbial mold. Brown hair falls in tousled waves around his head. The look is part carefree playboy, part romantic poet. Even from this distance, I can tell his body is insane. Muscular, big, and perfectly controlled in every movement.

And that's from being across the bar with less than stellar lighting.

A guy like that? There's no way he's the one who hasn't been able to take his eyes off me.

Lana is either fucking with me (unlikely) or trying to boost my confidence so that if Bro-Man tries to pick me up I'll feel good about myself. Lana is snarky, but never ever mean (at least not to me), so I doubt she's fucking with me. Trying to build up my confidence, however, is totally her jam.

Which is sweet of her, but unnecessary. I know I'm pretty enough. I have good hair when I bother to fix it. It's blonde, which, for some reason I've never understood, matters to some guys. And I'm blessed with the kind of curves that often garner a second look.

Catching the brief attention of a random guy in a bar has never been the problem. It's keeping that attention once the poor sap walks up to me. Once I open my mouth and start talking, I blow it by being too... well, too me.

Whatever mysterious, magical quality that allows some women to lure in men and hold their attention with sly looks and witty banter, I don't have it.

Lana has it. In spades.

I've seen men go from Can-I-buy-you-a-drink to You're-my-soulmate-will-you-marry-me in less than an hour with her. More than once.

It's just who she is.

And it's not who I am.

Maybe it's the neurospicy thing. Maybe it's something. But inevitably, when I open my mouth, I ruin it. Instead of banter, I end up talking about the geo-political implications of desertification in Africa. Or I point out a mole he should have checked. Once, I blurted that a guy reminded me of Snuffleupagus. I meant it as a compliment, but he took it the wrong way, and there's no coming back from that.

Somehow, even worse than my unique brand of man-repellent is that I'm never sorry when I've driven a man away. By the time they make excuses, it's a relief. Inevitably, I am as uninterested in them as they are in me. It's hardly my fault I can't tolerate men who are boring, self-absorbed twats.

This is something I've always been more at peace with than Lana has.

Still, I know she means well and that her concerns about the cobwebs in my lady garden might be valid. Yes, there's a certain efficiency in my ... um ... toys, but every once in a while it would be lovely to achieve orgasm with someone capable of snuggling afterwards.

I sigh, looking at Mr. Hot Young Thing.

Hell, even if he doesn't want to snuggle after, this creature is beautiful enough that it hardly matters.

All of that flashes through my mind before he even glances in my direction.

Then, his eyes raise and meet mine, and it feels like a jolt of electricity shoots through me. He stands from his bar stool, says something to the women and then walks around them—to head to me. What is happening right now?

I will kill Lana if she set this up.

I glance around the bar and see my friend talking to one of the servers as she mixes a colorful drink.

"I was wondering when you were going to feel the weight of my stare and look over."

The rich baritone voice is lined with just the hint of a Texas accent. The only thing sexier might be a British accent. Dammit.

I turn to face him, and wow—I was so not prepared.

Not for him up close. Not for him in all his sculpted handsomeness.

He flashes me a sexy grin. "I don't think I've ever gotten that reaction before." He must see my confusion because he adds, "the wow."

"Did I say that out loud?"

"You did."

Well, I guess it's better than comparing him to a Muppet.

He is younger, Lana was right about that. Maybe in his early twenties. Clearly too young for me.

"If Lana put you up to this or if you are planning to use this interaction for a dare or to win a bet, then keep on walking."

He sits on the stool next to me. Well, not so much sits as he kinda leans his butt against it. His t-shirt clings to his muscular torso like a damn lover.

Awesome, never been jealous of a shirt before. *Who is this guy*?

He points at himself. "This guy?"

"I seem to be speaking my thoughts, which is just going to make this disastrous," I say. *Or perhaps I should say, more disastrous than unusual.*

"Nah, Dimples, I'm thinking you're delightful, not disastrous in the least." He opens his arms as if inviting me in for a hug.

Delightful? Well, that's new.

Thank God I don't jump into his arms.

"What do you wanna know?"

"How old are you?"

"Twenty-seven."

"You sure about that? You look closer to twenty-one or barely twenty," I say.

"I'm sure. I've got a babyface. My twin brother—fraternal—has always called me that. Annoying fucker," he mutters.

I turn my body more to face him. And I think I'm probably smiling. "Tell me three things about yourself, but not your job or your name."

"Alright. I think The Mummy is the greatest movie of all time. I'm good with my hands. And I love animals."

"Which Mummy movie?" I ask, ignoring the other two items he ticked off on his fingers.

He frowns at my question. "No disrespect to Mr. Cruise, he's excellent in other movies. And while his Mummy movie wasn't bad, it's simply not The Mummy with Rick and Evie and Imhotep and Ardeth Bay. That's the greatest movie of all time."

"You feel pretty strongly about that," I say.

"I do. I even have a tattoo in honor of it. Wanna see?" He half turns his body, lifting part of his shirt as if he's gonna flash me his ink.

That makes me laugh. "Do you always flirt with women like this?"

He shakes his head. "No."

"What about your previous entourage?" I nod to where he was sitting earlier.

"Those women? Nah, they came up to me so I chatted with them, but they're not my type."

"Because you don't like beautiful women?"

"I, in fact, do like beautiful women, which is why I'm now here talking to you."

"Smooth. But I'm not buying it."

"I have time to convince you. Why don't you tell me your three things?"

"Same rules?"

"Sure."

"Okay. Well, I was born and raised in Connecticut. I'd much rather be hot than cold. And I think shrimp Pad Thai is the best thing I've ever had in my mouth."

It's not until he smirks that I realize what I said could be twisted into something sexual, but he doesn't bother grasping at my low-hanging fruit.

"Do you have strong opinions about movies?" he asks.

"Of course. Doesn't everyone?"

He lifts one of those muscular shoulders. "Some people are weird and don't like movies."

"People are weird," I agree.

"Cough it up, Dimples. Tell me what your favorite movie is."

I should probably be embarrassed by how much his charm is working on me, but instead, I just smile. "Favorite movie," I say, "I think I'd have to go with The Shawshank Redemption."

"Bullshit!" Lana says. Because, of course, that's when she'd walk back over to me.

The sexy man's chuckle is authentic, and he winks at me. "Busted."

I roll my eyes and shoot a glance at my friend. "You don't know everything about me."

"Pretty sure I do," Lana says without missing a beat. Then she points at the hot guy. "Her favorite movie is The Mummy."

I close my eyes. She just had to go there.

"Is that so?" he asks. "Well, Dimples, it looks like you and I have all sorts of things in common."

"Everyone likes that movie," I argue.

"Same favorite movie. I think you're sexy. You think I'm sexy."

"I never said that," I say.

"Just going by the 'wow' from before," he says.

"He's got you there, sugar tits," Lana says. "She totally thinks you're sexy," she says directly to him.

"I'm going to give you a pass on the movie

thing," he says. "Because Shawshank is a great film." Somehow he's standing closer to me and his hot breath is against my neck.

I shiver. My nipples harden.

"I think we should be honest with each other though. There's some incredible chemistry brewing between us. I felt it the moment I first saw you and your mouthwatering soft curves."

"What are you proposing?" I find myself asking, because for once, somehow, I haven't driven a man away merely by being myself, and he doesn't seem like a boring, self-absorbed twat.

"If I thought you'd agree to marry me, I'd whisk you off to Vegas or Jamaica and make it happen."

Lana walks off to mix another drink.

"But I'm guessing that's asking too much," he says, "so instead I would take a night. One night to make you forget the real world and let a man worship your body."

One finger trails down my arm, and I shiver in response. "How do I know I can trust you?"

He stands to his full height so he can look directly at me. "Do you want to see my ID? I have a download of my last medical tests, I'm clean on everything." He pulls his wallet out. "My name is—"

I put a finger to his lips and shake my head.

So far, all the things we said—and not said—have been perfect.

If we keep talking, either I'll blow it or he will.

Sure, there's a very good chance that this guy is not as great as he seems. But right now, I don't want to know that.

"Tonight let's be Rick and Evie. Let's not complicate it with our real lives."

He gives me a devastating smile, and my heart thumps in response.

"Alright, Evie, what do you say? Can I take you back to my place and do wicked things to you?"

I fold my lips in on themselves and consider his offer. I want to say yes. I never say yes to these sorts of things. Well, I'm rarely asked, but in those situations, I've never said yes. Growing up, I never snuck out of my house to meet friends and dabble with alcohol or weed. I've slept with exactly one guy, and we were in a relationship.

My eyes flit to Lana, and she's staring at me, nodding. "Do it," she mouths.

"Okay, Rick," I say. "Here's what we're going to do. You're going to leave your wallet here with my friend, Lana, on the off chance that my body is found chopped into little pieces."

His lips quirk with a smile, but he slaps his wallet on the bar top. "Let's go, Dimples."

chapter two

EVAN

The bartender shoots me a glare. "Don't make me regret encouraging this."

Her meaning is clear. She's got her girl's back and will mess me up if things don't go well. I'm former special forces. I know when someone is bluffing about their ability to inflict pain and when they're not. This chick is not bluffing.

Which isn't a problem since my only intention for the night involves making her friend come as many times as possible.

I put my hand on "Evie's" lower back and give the bartender a nod. "Promise she's in good hands," I say.

The bartender snorts.

When we step outside of Martini's, the curvy blonde stops walking. She looks up at me, apprehension all over her face. I move my hand.

"You can change your mind, beautiful," I tell her.

"It's just I've never done this sort of thing before, so I don't even know how to proceed."

I rub the back of my neck self-consciously. "I've never done this either."

She gives me a disbelieving look. "Isn't this just a regular Friday night for you?"

"It's actually a Wednesday night, and no."

Her eyes narrow. "You look like the kind of guy who has left a trail of broken hearts behind him."

"I hope I haven't," I say truthfully. When she still looks like she doesn't believe me, I continue. "I've spent the bulk of my twenties traveling." Leaving out pertinent details is challenging.

"To monasteries?" she asks.

That makes me laugh. "Not quite." We're just standing in the parking lot at the moment.

"Let me just try something," she says.

She leans up on her tiptoes and kisses me. It's pretty chaste, all things considered. But having her this close to me… feeling the impossible softness of her lips, inhaling the spicy scent of her, I am lost to this woman. I reach up, cup her cheek and slant my mouth across hers.

The first brush of our tongues feels like I've been plugged into an electrical circuit. Her fingers grab onto the front of my shirt and she whimpers into my mouth.

I've never gotten this hard this fast. But I don't want to lose control. I want to enjoy every moment I get to touch her. I force myself to break the kiss, then lean my forehead against hers.

"Is your place far from here?" she asks.

I want to pump my fist in the air. "I'm staying in one of the houses that overlooks the lake."

She grabs my hand and tugs. "Let's go."

"Are we in a hurry now?" I ask.

"I've never gotten wet from a kiss before. I'm counting on you having other skills."

I love that she speaks so boldly. I grab her hand and press it to the front of my jeans. "You've already made me so damn hard."

Her eyes flash, and her fingers curl around my denim-clad erection.

"Where's your car?" she asks.

I point to my truck parked a few spots away.

"I'll follow you," she says, then she heads to a small sedan.

I jump in my truck and less than ten minutes later, we're both parked in the driveway at the lake house. I grab her hand and lead her to the front door. While she steps inside and sets down her purse, I deal with turning off the alarm system.

"Gorgeous view," she says, standing at the wall of windows overlooking the lake.

I know what it looks like out that window, so instead, I'm looking at her when I agree with her.

"Stunning view," I say, my eyes locked on her ass.

"You're not even looking!"

I give her a grin and shrug. "I've seen that view, I was enjoying this one." I saunter to her.

"You are ridiculous," she says.

"Nah, Dimples. You just have a spectacular ass."

"Do you have condoms?" she asks.

There's no reason to tell her that this is my brother's vacation home, so there are likely condoms in every room. Maybe even in the refrigerator.

"Yeah, I have some in the bedroom."

"Where is the bedroom?" she asks. "I don't wanna lose my nerve." Her eyes quickly drag down and back up my body. "You are really sexy."

"You think I'm sexy?" I ask.

She rolls her eyes at me. "You," she pokes me in the chest.

I take the opportunity to grab her hand. She visibly swallows.

"You even said that back at the bar."

I keep her hand trapped against my chest and take a step closer to her. "Back at the bar, I was trying to convince the beautiful woman to come home with me."

"Well, you succeeded," she says. "I'm here."

"Before we do anything, I want you to know that I know you don't owe me anything, so no pressure or whatever."

"Are you changing your mind about tonight? About me?"

"Fuck no. I'd like to tear your damn clothes off and bend you over the couch. But like I said, this is new for me."

I put my other arm around her body and pull her flush, our other hands still trapped between our bodies.

"I've never seen a woman for the first time and immediately envisioned her naked and underneath me. I don't want to fuck this up."

This close to me, I can clearly see that her pupils are blown. Her breathing is labored, judging from the way her chest is moving against me.

"You're doing just fine." She shifts our bodies slightly, then takes my hand down her chest, and slips my fingers under the waistband of her pants and into her panties. "I don't think I've ever been this wet."

I move my fingers closer to her core until I find her slickness.

"Goddamn it, beautiful. You're drenched."

"Yes," she says. "Stop being careful with me. I've said yes, now take me."

Fuck, she's sexy. And so real and soft.

I plunge one of my digits into her hot channel, and she clasps onto my forearm.

"Bedroom?" she asks.

"Bedroom is up that staircase." I nod, indicating the stairs to our left that lead up to the owner's suite. It has a massive bed that overlooks the lake, and it's ridiculously comfortable. Any time I've ever stayed here, I've been reminded that Abel, my twin brother, could not have managed to sleep in the places I've slept. On the front lines, on loud as fuck helicopters, in crowded barracks. You learn to sleep when you can, so comfort hasn't been high on my list for years.

I wish I knew her real name. Because I already know once with this woman won't be enough. I was only partly kidding when I said I'd take her away tonight to get married. There's something about her that draws me in like the proverbial moth to the flame. Her plump curves caught my attention first. The way her jeans hugged those rounded hips and her ripe peach. In truth, I've never wanted to bite a woman on the ass, but I am dying to sink my teeth into the fleshy part of hers.

I pull my hand out of her panties and immediately lick her arousal off my finger. "Fucking delicious. Get your spectacular ass up those stairs and undress. You might want to get comfortable before I spend the next hour with my face between your thighs."

She gasps, but then turns and jogs up the stairs.

I'm struck by the urge to chase her, hunt her down, and take her wherever we land. I've never been particularly aroused by that primal need to hunt, but with her, I want to take her in every way possible.

I stalk up the stairs and find her already lying on the bed, her clothes scattered on the floor. I pull off my shirt, then take care of my shoes so I'm wearing only my jeans.

"Watching you run away like that," I wipe a hand down my face. "Made me want to chase you, hold you down, and fuck you raw." I can't even believe what I'm saying. I've never talked to a woman like this, but Dimples is different.

"Yes, you could do that. Honestly, I think I'd let you do just about anything to me."

I unbutton my jeans, letting the denim part, exposing my boxer briefs. I move over to the bedside table and check the drawer and find some condoms. I fish some out and drop them on the bed.

Her brows raise. "Think we'll need that many?"

"Maybe. I'm insatiable for you."

"You might change your mind after we do it once," she says.

I chuckle. "Impossible. I have a feeling there will never be enough with you." I crawl over her on the bed, bracing my arms on either side of her. "I'm going to eat your sweet pussy, Dimples, but before that, I need these lips."

I lower my mouth to hers and kiss her. Her tongue meets mine stroke for stroke, and her arms come around my body. We kiss like this, frenzied and hot, until my dick is leaking in my boxer briefs. So I start kissing my way down her body. Nibbles at her collarbones, down to her breasts. I spend time here, sucking one nipple into my mouth and then the other until she's writhing under me, mumbling incoherent words and begging me to fuck her.

I continue my journey down her body, nipping at her soft, rounded belly. This close and I can smell her arousal. I inhale deeply and growl.

"You smell like a dream," I tell her. Finally, I shoulder my way between her thighs. "Dimples, look at this pretty kitty. Goddamn it, woman." I'm out of patience, so I just dive in, licking up her folds, but careful to avoid her clit. At least for the moment.

Her tangy slick coats my tongue as I go. Then her fingers are threading through my hair, grabbing, pulling.

"Oh my God. Oh my God," she chants.

I rock myself into the mattress, desperate for some friction against my dick. I want to propose again, but this time for real. I don't know what it is about this woman, but she makes me think of forever.

Her pelvis bucks underneath me, and I press an arm over her hips to keep her where I want her. I want her to come on my tongue. I want her to scream my name, but she doesn't even know it.

I circle my tongue around her clit.

"Right there. Oh my God."

Nails scrape over my scalp, and I suck her clit into my mouth.

Her body tightens, then her release quakes through her. I keep my mouth on her until her body stills. She's breathing hard.

"I need another one," I tell her.

"What?" she asks.

I lock my eyes on hers and then slide two fingers inside her.

Her back arches off the bed.

I pump them in and out a few times before curving my fingers. When I brush them across that special spot, she nearly levitates.

"Oh damn!" she screams.

"There it is," I say. Then I lick her again while moving my fingers.

She makes a strangled noise in her throat. "What—" but her question dies as I double down on my work.

I keep my rhythm steady as I work my fingers and mouth. She's bucking underneath me, and fuck, I'm so damn hard I might come with her.

"It's too much," she whines.

But it's not, she can take it and give me even more.

Then she screams as she shatters and squirts all over my hand. I lap up all of her juices, then stand from the bed. I shuck the rest of my clothes and grab a condom to roll over my dick.

"You're so fucking sexy," I tell her. I line myself up at her entrance and slowly slide in all the way to the hilt.

"Holy fuck, Dimples, you feel so goddamn perfect."

"I think you're going to kill me," she says. Her legs hike up and wrap around my waist.

It sinks me a little deeper inside her.

"I just want to make you feel pleasure," I tell her.

"Death by pleasure," she says.

"I've got you, beautiful. I won't let you die."

I start to move then, sliding in and out of her hot, wet center.

"Christ, woman, you might just kill me with pleasure. You feel incredible."

"Yes," she hisses. Her chants of "Oh my God" continue.

"That's it. Want you to come all over my cock. Think you can do that?"

She shakes her head. "No."

"You're going to. I can feel how you're tightening around me. Squeezing me so good. Fuck, I'm not going to last. I need you to get there." I slide my hand between our bodies and find her clit.

That's all it takes.

"Coming!" she screams.

I let go, and then I'm coming too.

"I think you really are going to have to marry me," I say as I collapse beside her.

chapter **three**

MARLEY

Four months ago...

Even before I saw the two pink lines, I knew that night would live with me forever.

How could it not? He had been everything. An unparalleled lover, and I didn't need more experience to know that.

My first ever one-night-stand, and he'd forever changed me. Yes, because of the baby, but it was more than that. Somehow, in the midst of two strangers connecting in the most carnal of ways, he had somehow burrowed so deep into my conscious. I didn't even know his name, but there hadn't been a day in the last couple of months that I hadn't thought of him. He was my first thought every morning and my last before I went to sleep.

When I first found out I was pregnant, I tried to find him. He deserved to know. Lana didn't know who he was. I guess she's not as nosy as I am because had I had access to his wallet, I likely would have snooped on at least his name. And verified his age.

No one had answered the few times I'd knocked on that lake house door. It was probably an Airbnb, and I'd never find out his identity. I hated that for our child.

I'd grown up without a father, and it made me feel terrible that I'd created the same situation for my baby. But unless he just walked into my life, I had no idea how we could reunite.

chapter **four**

EVAN

"Explain it to me one more time," Abel says.

I stare at my brother. "Has Hollywood made you stupid? I'm not speaking a different language here. I've already told you."

He waves a hand dismissively. "Yeah, you said you were moving to some small town to run a dog park."

"For fuck's sake." I pinch the bridge of my nose. "You do not listen."

"I listen," he argues. "I heard that you're still hung up on some chick you banged months ago." He points at me. "Move on, brother, she's gone."

His words scrape against me like abrasive fabric. "Fuck off."

"Look, if you need money or whatever, you can work for me. Be my assistant. I can pay you more than enough."

"Are you fucking with me right now?"

He holds his hands up. "No. Just trying to help."

"It's like you don't even know me. I don't want to work for you. I don't want to move to Hollywood. I don't need money. I'm still thinking about the woman from that one night because she was special. I knew it then, and I should've done something about it. Like get her actual name. And I am not going to work at a dog park. It's a dog sanctuary where we rescue, rehabilitate, and rehome dogs. If you're itching to get rid of some of your cash, make a donation to the sanctuary."

Abel stares at me, his face as familiar as my own, despite the fact that we're not identical. "I hear you, Evan. Sorry. I'm just tired." He shakes his head. "I'll definitely make a donation."

I nod. "Thank you."

"What have you done to try to find the girl?"

"Went back to the bar and talked to the bartender—or she might be the owner, I'm not sure. In any case, she's friends with Dimples, but she refused to give me any additional details. Something about girl code."

"When was this?" Abel asks.

"The following day. After I woke up to an empty bed. I had to wait a while for the damn bar to open. Plus, she had my wallet. So I grabbed that, but she wouldn't give me any more information."

"Maybe you'll find each other again. If it's meant to be or whatever."

I snort. "You've been reading too many rom-com scripts."

chapter five

EVAN

Current day...

UNKNOWN NUMBER: Is this the number for Sergeant Cartwright?

ME: Sure is

ME: But I'm retired, so you can just call me Evan

ME: Who is this?

UNKNOWN NUMBER: Sorry. I'm just trying to be respectful.

UNKNOWN NUMBER: This is Dr. Olsen, the small animal vet. I just wanted to touch base with you about the appropriate protocols for those vaccines I sent over.

ME: Hey, Doc! Nice to meetcha.

ME: Thanks for helping out with the vaccines for all the pups at Great Danes!

DR. OLSEN: You're welcome.

DR. OLSEN: Those vaccines need to be stored at the proper temperatures until you're ready to use them.

ME: Yep. I got them stashed in the fridge as soon as they arrived.

DR. OLSEN: Please tell me you're NOT storing them in your home refrigerator. I was told you would have a medical refrigerator at the rescue center.

ME: Yeah. We do. That's where they are.

DR. OLSEN: And they're being kept within the proper temperature range?

DR. OLSEN: I can't guarantee their potency if they're allowed to sit out and then recooled. Or worse, accidentally freeze.

ME: Well, I did store them on top of the microwave for a bit, but that was just to make room for the keg. I put them back once the party started.

DR. OLSEN: What???

DR. OLSEN: Maybe I should come over there. Handle things myself.

ME: I'm joking!

ME: Jesus, have you met Dane? He'd kill any of us if we so much as stash our lunch in the fridge.

DR. OLSEN: This isn't a laughing matter. Administering unsafe vaccines would be extremely dangerous.

DR. OLSEN: And, yes, of course I've met Dane. I wouldn't have sold him the vaccines without my supervision if I didn't trust him.

ME: Don't worry. I've got this.

ME: I was a medic. I assure you, I know what I'm doing.

DR. OLSEN: A medic?

ME: In the Army. I'm trained in emergency wound care, among other things.

DR. OLSEN: Emergency wound care on humans is not the same thing as veterinary care. Maybe I should come out to supervise.

ME: That's not necessary, Doc.

DR. OLSEN: I'm attaching a PDF that includes detailed instructions on how to administer the medications.

ME: I've got it.

DR. OLSEN: And here are links to instructional videos if the PDF is too long.

ME: I said, I've got it. And the PDF is only three pages. With pictures. And I can read.

I groan aloud. What is up with that woman?

I switch out of the texting window with Dr. Olsen and over to the group text between me and my buddies who all run Great Dane's Dog Sanctuary.

I'm annoyed. I can't deny that.

First of all, I'm not used to people not liking me. I'm an affable guy. Secondly, she just straight up questioned my ability to not only read simple directions but to follow through with the job. I'm pretty sure that at most veterinary offices, vet techs are allowed to administer injections. Surely my education and subsequent experience give me at least that much skill. Maybe I shouldn't have made that joke about having a kegger, but come on! It was obviously a joke.

I blow out a breath, trying to release my annoyance. It won't do anyone any good, especially me, if I'm all worked up.

I try to focus on the string of texts from my buddies. They've apparently been chatting while I've been defending my honor to the lady vet.

LIAM: Thanks for not being total asshats when I brought Wren and Keller by today.

JACK: When are we ever asshats?

DANE: That might apply to everyone but you, Jack.

JACK: Does that make me the pussy of the group?

DANE: No. Just the golden retriever.

ROMEO: Dane is not wrong.

ROMEO: Your bird girl is perfect for you.

BEAU: Bird girl?

LIAM: Romeo is just being his hilarious self.

ROMEO: Because her name is Wren. Like a bird.

BEAU: That's weak, dude.

FLYNN: You can bring Keller out anytime. That kid is smart.

DANE: Why am I not surprised that the two of you hit it off?

FLYNN: What does that mean?

JACK: I think it's a two birds of a feather comment.

FLYNN: For me and Keller? I'll take it.

LIAM: He's an amazing kid. I'll be proud to call him my son.

ROMEO: You doing that legally or just claiming him with your words?

LIAM: Legally. Blake is working on the petition of adoption now.

DANE: That's great. Congrats.

ROMEO: Where's the kid?

JACK: Yeah, he normally lives for these group chats.

DANE: Evan! WTF are you?

ME: I'm here. Sorry. What did I miss?

FLYNN: What are we missing?

ME: What?

ROMEO: Yeah, what's going on with you, Kid? You've been in a shit mood for months.

This is when I could open up to my closest friends and tell them about my night with the woman of my dreams. Known only to me as "Evie" or Dimples, and presumably out of my life like a phantom. I could probably ask Flynn to see if he could work some computer magic to find her for me. But truthfully, I don't have enough information to go on. Besides, she made it clear she wanted only one night. I have too much dignity to chase someone who doesn't want to be chased. And I respect all women enough to back off if they're not interested. So instead, I skip my romantic woes and complain about the veterinarian.

ME: It's that fucking vet bossing me around like I don't know what the hell I'm doing. I was a special forces medic for fuck's sake. I think I can handle a few canine vaccinations.

DANE: Uh-oh.

ROMEO: You are so screwed, my brother.

FLYNN: <gif of cupid shooting off an arrow>

ME: I hope you're not suggesting that I'm into her.

BEAU: We would never.

ME: Seriously, she's not even nice to me. Also, I haven't even met her.

ME: She could be a 65-year-old woman.

ME: I just don't get what I could have done to warrant her hostility.

ME: She's questioned everything.

ME: And she sent me a how-to video!

ME: To give an injection!

ME: She's clearly just a grouch. I mean, really, have y'all ever met a grumpy veterinarian?

JACK: Well, they do have to deal with some tough situations.

BEAU: Exactly. They lose patients too.

ME: I wasn't talking about that.

ME: She essentially gets to cuddle dogs and cats all day. Aside from the hard parts, that shit should make you smile.

ROMEO: Haven't seen you smiling around all the dogs.

FLYNN: He's not wrong.

LIAM: You've been in a bad mood, Kid. If you can't deal with the lady doctor, we can transfer that role to someone else.

LIAM: Romeo could do it.

ROMEO: Romeo is busy trying to get the piece of shit second-hand van we bought up and running.

LIAM: Minor details.

ME: I can work with her.

ME: I am a professional!

ME: She's the grumpy, mean one.

Maybe what I need to do is just go down to her office and introduce myself. Once she's met me in person, I'm sure she'll relax and feel more comfortable with my skills.

And as if Dane—essentially my boss—is reading my mind, he sends me a private text.

DANE: What's going on, Kid? It's not like you to not be able to get along with someone.

DANE: It just makes the most sense for you to be the one to handle the most pressing canine medical needs.

ME: I've got it. I'm going to go meet her.

ME: Everyone likes me. Surely, I can convince the old bat to trust me a little.

DANE: I don't think she's as old as you're imagining.

ME: Whatever. I can charm her.

ME: I've got this, Dane. Promise.

DANE: Be sure that you do. The logistics of getting Marley out to the sanctuary every time we need vaccinations sounds like a nightmare.

DANE: And I don't even want to think about bringing them all to her.

DANE: Especially with our van in and out of the shop as much as it has been.

ME: I can ask Abel to buy us a new one. It would be a tax write-off for him.

DANE: We don't need your movie star brother to buy us anything. Besides, if that's all it took, remember my sister-in-law is Jess Munoz.

DANE: She probably has more money than your brother.

ME: I've seen footage of her sold- out concerts. She probably does have more money.

DANE: So you've got this?

ME: Yes. You can count on me.

ME: I'll find a way to win over the veterinarian.

chapter six

MARLEY

The only thing that would make today worse is if I had the puppy vomit in my hair rather than just on my scrubs. Poor little guy had gotten into a bag of charcoal and then became a canine volcano.

Thus is the glamorous life of a small-town veterinarian.

Don't get me wrong, I love my job. I would much rather spend copious amounts of time with the four-legged than any of the other two-legged and talking variety. And I especially love this time of day, when the appointments are over, the chaos has quieted, and I'm (mostly) alone.

I've already sent all the techs home for the day, and it's just me in the back finishing up some patient notes, and Dylan, our receptionist, is out front. He could have already gone home, but he never lets me stay here alone. His sweet Texas boy manners won't let him leave me on my own.

I think back to my earlier text exchange with Sergeant Cartwright. As if learning how to bandage wounds is the same thing. Not to mention that canine anatomy is very different than human.

I'll have to revisit my previous conversation with Dane Whitmore, the owner of the dog sanctuary. Initially agreeing to hand over the vaccinations to the guys who work there made sense. It was a partnership I didn't see coming when I first moved to Saddle Creek nearly six months ago. The former military unit turned dog rescuers have created something really special out at their facility and land. Especially as they grow in popularity and continue to take in more and more dogs.

It's not that I can't drive out there myself to administer the vaccinations, but that would consume a good chunk of my time. So when Dane contacted me to tell me that one of his buddies who had moved here to run the sanctuary with him had been the team—unit—whatever they're called, the one who had some medical training. Needless to say, at the time, it had seemed like a great solution for both of us.

He might not know anything specifically about canine anatomy, but at least he'll know his way around a syringe. That's truly the most difficult part. But then, when I texted him and he was talking about the keg and the fridge, he just did not seem like he was taking the issue seriously at all.

And, yes, I know I tend to take everything seriously. Still, it's my attention to detail that makes me a great vet, and I refuse to apologize for that.

My eye catches on the framed ultrasound picture sitting on my desk. I smile, looking at the grainy image. My hand falls to my bump and I pat the life growing inside me. If you had told me last year this time that I'd be pregnant, I would have laughed in your face.

All it takes is that one time. Isn't that what everyone tells teenagers?

Evidently, it applies to thirty-something single women, too. And technically, it could have been one of *three* times we'd done it that night. Though admittedly, it was all in one night, so I'm not sure any of those details matter.

I don't look pregnant to most people yet because I'm plus- sized. I already had a soft belly. But I know the difference. I can feel the difference, inside and out. Maybe I just look fatter to other people, but I know that a life is nestled inside me, growing and changing every day.

The number of times his handsome face has come to mind over the last few months is embarrassing. Especially since I have no way of contacting him to tell him, 'hey, you're gonna be a dad.'

How would that even go anyways?

Remember me? Your one-night stand? We didn't exchange names or contact information, but it would seem that despite using condoms, you knocked me up!

I blow out a breath. Some of the blonde fuzzies currently surrounding my face flutter. Today's humidity has my pale locks frizzed to the extreme. I'm pretty sure it looks more like my head is covered in yellow cotton candy than actual hair.

But again, no dog vomit in said hair, so I'm calling it a win.

Dylan's friendly voice catches my attention at the front desk. Might be an emergency since it's past appointment time. So I pull myself up to go out and see what's going on.

How I can already have a sore back at only five months pregnant is beyond me. But since I'm considered geriatric in my pregnancy because of my advanced age, I've been instructed to take things as physically easy as possible.

That means no more lifting sixty-five-pound dogs up on a table, which is admittedly a pain in the ass.

I step out into the lobby and then stop in my tracks when I see him. *Him*, him. My hand falls to my baby bump again.

How can *he* just be standing there?

In my vet clinic?

Talking to my receptionist as if this isn't complete insanity?

"What are you doing here?" I hear myself ask.

"Came to introduce myself to the vet—" That's when my mystery man—my baby daddy —looks up and sees me, but there's no recognition in his face.

Does he not recognize me? Am I so forgettable that standing this close to me, he doesn't immediately know me? I have an entire catalogue of memories about him from our one night together. The scar on his lower hip. The tattoos on his back—including the one from *The Mummy*. The way he growled the nickname *Dimples* when he came. Every. Single. Time.

Shit!

I frown. No. This is not happening. "I have to talk to Dane. There's been a change in plans. I'll talk to him. You just... you go." I ramble and then turn to go back into the back, but run directly into a display of metal collar tags.

"Dylan, can you grab that? I have an emergency I've got to run to." Then I just leave. Walk into the back and out the back door straight to my car.

Holy shit!

How did my baby daddy just walk into my veterinarian clinic? How did he not recognize me?

chapter seven

EVAN

I can't decide if I'm hallucinating or not. But I'm pretty sure that was my girl.

My girl.

Here.

Somehow, impossibly, she's here. My girl.

And I'm just standing here like an idiot, gaping at her.

Fuck.

I jump over the counter and run through the door where she disappeared.

Dylan, the receptionist, is hot on my heels. "You can't be back here."

But she's nowhere to be found, and when I open the back door, I see a car pulling out of the parking lot.

"Fuck!"

"Dude, really, you can't be back here," Dylan says.

I walk past him, hands held up. "Got it. I'm leaving."

I climb into my truck and fire up the engine. Mentally, I play back what happened in the vet clinic.

What is she doing here?

Obviously, my Dimples is the vet.

Dr. Olsen.

The same woman who's been a thorn in my side for the last twenty-four hours. With all her texting nonsense and how-to-videos. Fuck, she's cute.

But how is it even possible that she's the vet?

She'd asked what I was doing there. So did that mean she recognized me, but wasn't happy to see me?

Goddamn it, she better not fucking be married. Maybe she was just surprised.

"Fuck!" I roar. I bang my hands on the steering wheel.

But then something occurs to me. If Dimples is Dr. Olsen, Saddle Creek's small animal veterinarian, then that must mean she lives here.

Surely that's a sign. It's gotta mean that we're meant to be. How could it not mean that?

Had the hottest, best night of my life with the woman, and I haven't stopped thinking about her since. We belong together. This is proof.

I drive out to my place. Well, technically, it's not mine; it's my temporary dwelling. Dane has a tiny home he built that is so cool. Since he and Shelby built a house together, he's not living there, so we're currently using the downstairs space as Great Dane's Dog Sanctuary's main office. But that left the loft bedroom available.

We've got a nice working setup outside of the tiny house, too. That's where I find Romeo when I pull my truck up.

"Thank fuck you're here," I say as I get out of the vehicle.

He looks up from whatever he's whittling. His brows raise.

"What's going on, Kid?" he asks.

"I'm going to give you a quick history. A few months ago, I met a gorgeous woman and we spent one amazing night together. I haven't been able to stop thinking about her since, but we didn't exchange names. So there's been no way for me to find her. Well, guess what?"

"You found her?" he asks, drolly.

"She's the vet."

"The one you were complaining about earlier?"

"Yes. It was bothering me that she didn't seem to like me, considering we hadn't met in person. So I drove over to her clinic this afternoon, and there she was." I frown.

"What's wrong?"

"I don't know if she recognized me or not. She said something about not being able to do something and then ran out the back door."

"Sounds like she might have recognized you," my buddy says.

"You think?" I wipe a hand down my face. "I don't know. Regardless, doesn't it seem like it's a sign that we're meant to be, that we both live in the same small town?"

"I'm not one for signs and fate and all that," Romeo says. "But if you like this woman, then I say go for it. Ask her out. What's the worst that could happen?"

chapter eight

MARLEY

What is happening right now?

Well, first of all, I'm driving aimlessly. I just knew I needed to get out of there fast. I pull over on the side of the road and grab my phone.

I call Lana because she's the only one who knows about him. The hot guy from the bar. My "Rick" for the night. But her phone rolls straight to voicemail. She's probably working. I could drive there, but Crescent Bend is nearly two hours away.

Still, I need to talk to someone, so I push to call the one woman I've sort of bonded with since moving here. It's never been easy for me to make friends, and Shelby seems not to find me overwhelming or annoying. Or if she does, she hides it well.

"Hey, lady!" she says cheerfully when she answers.

"Hi. Quick question."

"Shoot."

"Are we good enough friends for me to have a total breakdown in front of you?"

"I'm pulling the ice cream out of the freezer as we speak. Come on over."

"Thank you, Shelby."

"Of course. And we are good enough friends," she assures me before we hang up.

It doesn't take me too long to drive out to her and Dane's place. It's on the same property as the dog sanctuary, but has a separate drive and entrance.

I've barely put my sensible sedan in park before I'm out the door and walking to their front door. Shelby meets me with a pint of ice cream and a spoon, then she leads me to the kitchen table.

That's one thing I noticed after moving to the south. People congregate in the kitchen.

Usually around a table, always with food and lemonade or sweet tea.

Shelby doesn't even ask, she just puts me in a chair and sets a glass of iced tea in front of me. I shove a spoonful of ice cream in my mouth, then immediately regret it because, well, it's really cold.

Once I get it swallowed, I ask, "You know how I told you that the baby daddy was just a one-night stand? And that I'd never see him again?"

Shelby stops mid-spoon-to-her-mouth. Her eyes go round. "Oh my God! Did you see him? Is it someone in town?"

"Yes. Well, I don't know, actually. I just know he showed up at my clinic this afternoon, and I freaked out and just left." I drop my head in my hands. "I mean, I literally ran out of my own office. Why did I just run away?"

"You were probably shocked, honey." She squeezes my hand. "Okay, so can you break it down a little more for me? Was he there to see you? Do you think he just found you?" Shelby asks.

"I can't imagine that. I mean, he might have

asked my friend Lana, but she wouldn't have told him without asking me first."

"Did he have an animal with him?"

I shake my head. "I don't think so. He and Dylan were just talking when I stepped out front. I thought it might be an emergency. I saw him and gah," I put a hand to my heart. "He's more beautiful than I remember him being. His hair is a little longer up top, too."

"Evan was just at your office," Dane says as he walks into the room. "He went to see you because I guess you were giving him a hard time about the vaccines." Shelby's husband chuckles, then kisses her on the head.

"Evan Cartwright." Shelby whistles. "Solid choice. He's definitely a hottie. And sweet as pie."

"Oh, you think Evan saw whoever this was that you recognized?" Dane asks. He turns a chair backwards and straddles it, facing the table.

That's when it all hits me, makes sense in my head. Evan Cartwright, as in Sergeant Cartwright, is one of Dane's guys. He's the medic I was giving crap to via text. My baby daddy doesn't just live here; I'm going to have to work with him.

I lay my head on the edge of the table and bang it gently.

"I can't believe this is happening," I murmur as I bang, bang, bang.

"No, Dane, you're missing the biggest detail," Shelby says. "Evan is the man she recognized. He's her baby daddy."

I peek over to see Dane's reaction.

Dane's light, congenial expression shifts into something darker. "Are you fucking with me right now?"

"No, she's right. Unless he has a twin. Oh wait, I think he said he had a twin that night, but that they weren't identical," I say.

"Fucking son of a bitch. I'm going to kick his ass." Dane is up, and the door slams as he runs out of the house.

Shelby blows out a breath. "He was a little slow to catch on to that one. Poor guy has been stressed lately. I think it's the speed at which the sanctuary is expanding. He's worried they can't keep up with the need. Especially with the recent fires in California. It's displaced a lot of dogs, and we're one of the only places that are accepting some."

Then she frowns.

"He won't really kick his ass, right?" I ask. "I mean, how much damage can two former soldiers cause to one another?" Even as I say the words, I know they're stupid.

Shelby bites down on her lip, then stands, puts the lids on the pints of ice cream, and tosses them in the freezer.

"Let's go make sure my man doesn't kill your man," she says. I follow her outside where she jumps into the golf cart parked in front of their house. "Hop in, it'll be faster this way." She passes her phone over to me. "You can see Dane's location there, just tell me where to go."

chapter
nine

EVAN

"She could say no," I say. "Oh fuck, what if she's married?"

Romeo opens his mouth to say something, but I continue with my thoughts. "No, she wouldn't do that. I know her. Even just from that one night, I know she's not the type of person to do that."

Romeo nods.

"Are you fucking kidding me?" a voice roars from behind me. I turn in time to see Dane charging towards me.

I don't even have time to ask him what he's talking about before he literally knocks me to the ground. The air whooshes out of my lungs.

"Dane! What the fuck?" Romeo yells.

"This moron doesn't know how to wrap his dick up," Dane says. Then he punches me.

I see stars as the pain radiates through my skull. "I don't know what's happening, but that fucking hurt!"

He's gripping my shirt in both of his hands.

"Didn't anyone ever teach you to wear condoms, you little shit?"

"Dane. What the hell are you talking about? I always use condoms."

"Then tell me how you managed to knock up Marley?" Dane yells.

"Who the hell is Marley?" I ask.

Dane rears his fist back like he's gonna hit me again, but thankfully, Romeo pulls him off.

"Brother, you need to calm down," Romeo says. He's got Dane's arms pulled behind. Romeo stares at Dane until their gazes meet. "You good?"

Dane's chest is rising rapidly with his labored breathing. He cracks his neck and shoots me another glare. "Yeah, I'm good."

I almost ask Romeo to keep holding the big guy away from me, but I don't want to seem like a total pussy. It's not that I can't fight, I can. And I'm good at it. But there's a reason I became a medic. My body might be honed and trained to deliver a beating, but it makes me physically ill to hurt someone.

It's what my mama always called my tender heart.

"Can you explain what's going on?" Romeo asks. "What has you so fired up?"

"The kid here," Dane nods towards me. "Got Shelby's friend, Marley, pregnant."

"I don't know anyone named Marley. And I sure as hell didn't get anyone pregnant!"

"I beg to fucking differ. She's over at my house right now in tears because you got her pregnant and then disappeared."

When I don't respond, Dane rolls his eyes.

"Marley Olsen. Are you telling me you got her pregnant and you don't even know her name?"

His words seem to echo through my head, bouncing off things and not settling. I take a deep breath, then go through the details as I know them. "Marley Olsen. Dr. Olsen. The veterinarian is pregnant. Marley is the veterinarian. Marley is my girl. Marley is pregnant with my child."

"Sit down, Evan," Romeo says from somewhere behind me. "You look like you're gonna pass out."

He steers me over to the covered picnic table that works as our office on days with nice weather. I sit and drop my head into my hands.

"A baby," I say. "I used a condom. Every single time. I've never not used a condom."

"Well, you fucked something up," Dane says. "You know you have to do right by her. You can't just walk away."

Those words, among any of the others he's slung at me, hit me straight in the chest. I stand and take a step towards one of my closest friends and the man who is currently my boss.

"Do you honestly think I wouldn't step up and do what's right? Obviously, I'm gonna do whatever I need to do to take care of her and this baby. I'll be damned if I walk out on my kid like my dad did to me."

"Both of you, calm down," Romeo says. "Dane, I'm sure Evan is going to do the right thing."

"Yes, of course. I'll marry her. I'll do the right thing. There's no way I'm going to let a kid of mine grow up a bastard."

"Not if I have a say in matters," her voice says from behind me.

chapter ten

MARLEY

I glare at the display of raw masculinity in front of me. In any other moment than this one—where I arrive in time to hear three adult men, one the husband of a friend, the second my baby daddy, and the third a stranger to me—when I hear them planning my life. Making my decisions. No, thank you.

Evan, at least now I know his name, steps towards me.

He holds his hand out. "We should've done this that night," he says.

I take his hand, and he captures mine in between both of his.

"Evan Cartwright." His voice is steady.

"Marley Olsen," I say.

"It is really fucking nice to meet you," he says, dropping my hand. He swallows visibly. "Are you really pregnant, Dimples?"

The question alone could rankle, especially because I'm sure I don't look it from most people's perspective. I just look as if I've been hitting the daily two-dollar special at the local ice cream parlor, Sprinkles, too often. But there's nothing but sincerity and... hope? Oh God, is that hope reflecting in his gaze? My emotions are knotted in my throat, so I don't dare speak; I just nod.

He steps even closer to me and holds his hands out. "May I?"

I'm not a hundred percent sure what, specifically, he's asking, but again, I just nod.

His big palms go to my lower belly and cradle it. Then he drops to his knees and leans his head against the swell of my belly.

Then he looks up at me, his green eyes filled with emotion. "Can they hear me?"

I clear my throat and pray that I'm not actually crying. "I talk to her, but I don't think she can hear quite yet."

"She? It's a girl?"

I nod. "I found out last week. All of her little parts are there and normal, and she's growing on track."

"A girl," he repeats.

It's then that I remember that we have an audience. We are not having this moment in a vacuum, nope, we're having it in front of Evan's co-workers and my only friend in town. I take a step back, breaking Evan's connection with my body.

"I want you to know that I tried to find you when I found out I was pregnant. To no avail, obviously. But now that you know, you can, of course, have full rights as her father. Once she's born, we can work out visitation or a custody agreement."

He stands, his brows heavy with a frown. "I don't want to be a part-time father," he growls.

The tone and weight of his indignation inexplicably turn me on. My nipples harden to almost painful tips and my entire lady garden blooms with need. Stupid hormones. And stupid hot man who just lights up my body.

"Well, I don't want to marry just because it's your duty or whatever nonsense you were spouting when I first walked up. I am not a Victorian debutante worried about her reputation. We are long past the time when a man *had* to marry a pregnant woman to salvage her in the eyes of the world."

"That is not what I meant," he says, his eyes practically glowing with ferocity. "I looked for you too, you know."

I roll my eyes. "No, you went back to the bar to retrieve your wallet and just asked Lana if she'd give you my name. It was a drive-by scenario, hardly worth mentioning."

"Y'all are giving me whiplash," Shelby announces. She comes closer to Evan and me. "This is not something that's going to be resolved with a casual chat. I think for now, maybe it's best if you separate and regroup, if you will."

I'm simultaneously annoyed and grateful that she interrupted us. Mostly grateful. Because as much as he's pretty to look at and he smells delicious, I evidently can't be near him right now until I get my thoughts lined up.

"Good idea," I muse. I turn to Shelby. "Could you take me back to my car?"

"Of course," Shelby says.

I look at Evan and give him a nod. "We'll talk again."

"But-" Evan tries to protest, the man I don't know silences him with a simple, "Kid."

I turn to go to the golf cart we arrived in. I see Shelby hang back for a minute, and she says something to Evan quietly so I can't hear.

"Dane, baby, keep your hands to yourself until you get home, please," she singsongs to her husband. "We don't need to further mess up Evan's pretty face.

chapter eleven

EVAN

I am not in the mood to meet with the guys right now, but I've been summoned to the VFW Hall, where we currently have our staff meetings. It's been a hell of a twenty-four hours. A life-changing twenty-four hours.

My phone rings and I see Abel's name flash up.

"It's about fucking time," I say as a greeting.

"Good morning to you, too, Mary Sunshine. What crawled up your ass and died?" My brother's voice comes through my truck's speakers.

"I called you like four times last night," I say. "Where were you?"

"Production meeting. Everything is a shit show here, but I'll figure it out. What's going on there?"

"I'm going to be a father," I blurt. Shit, I meant to ease into that part. Tell him about Marley.

"What?"

"A dad. You know, me, which I guess means you're going to be an uncle."

"You knocked someone up? Are you sure it's yours? Did you take a paternity test? Don't make any promises, verbal or otherwise, until you speak to an attorney. I can have one of mine call you," Abel says.

"Slow your roll, brother. No, I didn't take a paternity test, but yes, I'm sure it's mine."

"Have you been in an exclusive relationship you haven't told me about?"

"Well, no. But I know her. She wouldn't lie about anything, much less something this big."

My phone pings with an incoming text.

DANE: Meeting only works if you come inside and sit with us. Not stay in your fucking truck.

I blow out a breath.

"Abel, I gotta go. Work meeting. We can talk later, yeah?"

"Course. But promise me you'll talk to an attorney."

"I really don't think that's necessary."

"Evan, be serious, man. This girl could be—"

"What? After your money? She doesn't even know who you are. Or maybe she knows you, the movie star, but she doesn't know you're my brother."

He's still protesting when I disconnect our call. Yeah, Hollywood has not been good for Abel's trust issues. When you have a dad who only pops into your life when he needs something—primarily to borrow money—then you tend not to take people at their word. Abel and I handled our distrust in different ways.

I joined the Army and learned that you can

actually rely on some people. Abel ran off to Hollywood and became a blockbuster hit.

ABEL: Call my attorney. I'll share his contact info with you.

I roll my eyes as I get out of my truck and head inside the VFW. Sure enough, as soon as I step inside, I can easily see that the rest of the guys are already here and gathered around one of the large tables.

Per usual, Romeo is whittling something.

"About damn time," Dane mutters as I sit at the table.

"Give the kid a break," Romeo says.

"Dane filled us in a little on your situation," Liam says.

I shoot a glare at my boss. "Not your news to share," I mutter.

"Is it good news?" Jack asks.

"Yes, it's good news. I'm excited about the baby, but even more so to have found my girl," I say.

"I feel like we're missing details," Flynn says.

"Not a whole lot of details to share. We met in Crescent Bend, right before I moved down here. Shared an incredible night together. We had originally agreed on no names, but by the time I woke up the next morning, I was ready to give her my Social Security number, if she needed it. But she was already gone."

I shrug. "I tried to ask about her, but I knew next to nothing about her except that there was something special between us and I wanted more."

"So then what all happened yesterday?" Beau asks.

"You know the veterinarian was giving me a hard time yesterday via text. I decided I was going to go over there and meet her so she could feel more confident in my ability to administer the vaccines. But we never even got to that part. I walked in, saw her, and she ran away."

"She came to my house to see Shelby," Dane adds.

"And you kicked my ass without knowing the full story," I say.

He holds his hands up. "Look, I have a

younger sister. When girls cry, I act, that's just how it is."

"You thought I'd done it on purpose. Got her pregnant, that is."

"Incorrect. I thought you'd been a moron and hadn't worn a condom," Dane clarifies.

"Same fucking difference," I mutter.

"I'm sorry I jumped to conclusions," Dane says.

"And?"

"And I'm sorry I messed up your pretty face."

"Thank you."

"That is quite a shiner you've got," Flynn says.

"I suspected as much yesterday, watching you with her, but am I right to assume you want to be with Marley?" Dane asks. "Long term?"

"You know what's funny? I totally asked her to marry me that night. She never answered. Probably assumed I was joking, and maybe I was. But I think a part of me knew she was meant to be mine. The baby proves that."

"So then what's the problem?" Beau asks.

"She doesn't want to be with me," I say. "Or at least she doesn't want to be an obligation to me."

"That's easy enough to fix," Liam says.

All eyes turn to him.

"You just have to show up. Again and again. Eventually she'll believe that you mean what you say. That you're not going anywhere. And that you'll wait for her as long as she needs you to."

I nod. "I can do that."

"You bet your ass you can," Flynn says. "And we'll help."

chapter twelve

MARLEY

I came straight home after Shelby's, stopping only once to pick up a burger to go from Ace's Bar and Grill. I've never really been one for hamburgers, but these are ridiculously tasty, and I guess the baby needed some meat.

I'd devoured that and taken a shower and crawled into my bed, e-reader in hand, ready to disappear into the historical romance I'd been reading. All three cats had been piled on the bed with me. Even Ambrosia, my bitchy long-haired calico. She'd never been one for snuggling, but ever since I got pregnant, she joins the boys, Basil and Badger, on the bed.

Though she tends to stay down at my feet, whereas my sweet boys are closer to my head.

My phone had pinged. And pinged again. And then three more times. It was already plugged into the charger, and normally I had a no phone in my bed rule, but given the events of the day, I pick it up.

EVAN: Marley.

EVAN: It feels amazing to know your actual name now.

EVAN: Though you'll always be Dimples to me.

EVAN: You have no idea how happy I am that we've found each other again.

EVAN: Feels very serendipitous.

I'm smiling.

That's annoying that five simple text

messages from that man can make me smile so big that my cheeks hurt. He's so charming and—romantic. There's no other way to describe him. It felt that way in the lake house that night, but I'd chalked it up to just the whole spontaneity of the evening.

EVAN: Will you tell me more about the pregnancy? How you've been feeling?

EVAN: Are you taking enough folic acid?

EVAN: I really wish I'd been here from the beginning. When you first found out.

ME: Hi.

Wow, am I lame or what?

Hi, I'm Marley. I have no social skills. Even when texting.

Ridiculous.

EVAN: You're there.

ME: I'm here.

ME: I'm taking a prenatal vitamin my doctor prescribed me.

ME: Since I'm considered geriatric for pregnancy, they're watching me closely.

EVAN: Geriatric? That's ridiculous.

ME: Anyone woman over 35 is considered to be in that category.

EVAN: You're not geriatric. But I'm glad you're getting good prenatal care.

EVAN: Can I come with you to the next doctor's appointment?

ME: Sure.

We'd gone back and forth like that for over an hour. Talking about nothing and the pregnancy. I ignored all his flirtatious comments and tried not to like him more than I already did before he popped back up in my life. That seems like a futile battle.

After we'd concluded our texting conversation, my body had been so alert, so on edge, that I'd had to pull out my favorite toy to relieve some tension. We hadn't discussed anything sexy, but just he was out there, in the same town as me. And imagining the sound of his deep voice, edged with that Texas twang had me all kinds of riled up.

The cats had deserted me when I'd turned on the vibrator, but they'd come back eventually. It had made me wonder if Evan liked cats. He'd told me that first night that he loved animals, but there were a lot of animal lovers out there who put cats in the same category as spiders.

Now, the following morning, I stare, bleary-eyed, out my front window at my pretty little fenced-in yard. That white-picket fence that borders my yard and all the pretty little window boxes are what sold this house for me. At the time, I'd had delusions of grandeur about my ability to nurture plants.

I'm good with animals, so it seemed logical I'd be good with plants. The reality is, not so much. Thankfully, I've got several crepe myrtles that flourish in the hot, dry Texas summer. So their pretty and brightly colored blooms are hopefully hiding the fact that I killed everything else in the yard.

I take another slow sip of my coffee—half caffeine, half decaf—because I'm trying to be good for baby girl's sake. I had a rough night sleeping and feel as if I'm barely functioning this morning. Thankfully, it's my day off, so I can move as slowly as I want to. Maybe I won't even change out of my pajamas.

Something catches my eye on the left side of my yard. There's a truck parked along the street across from my house. I've never officially met that neighbor, but I've heard they hate it when people park in front of their house.

If it wasn't a thousand degrees outside, I'd go sit on my front porch just to watch that little old lady scold whoever was foolish enough to park on their street. I snicker to myself, then frown when I see the driver get out.

"What is he doing here?" I mutter.

Basil is the one that chirps a response. My pretty Siamese has always been the talker of my crew. Ambrosia is much more comfortable glaring from whatever perch she's balanced herself on. And Badger, well, he's an orange tabby with all the lunacy that comes with orange cats.

I blow out a breath, then set my coffee down and walk outside. I suppose it would be only right if I warned my baby's daddy that he shouldn't park in front of that particular neighbor's house.

But when I step out on my porch, I get the full view of my yard, which now includes a blue pop-up tent.

"What in the actual fuck?"

"Oh good, you're awake," he says, walking towards me. He's got one of those cup carriers in one hand, holding four to-go drinks, and has a bright pink bag in his other hand. I recognize immediately that the drinks are from The Coffee Cup, and that pink bag is definitely from Sugar Bakers, the local bakery.

It never occurred to me that my white picket fence isn't very tall until I see Evan and his sexy, long legs merely step over the wood slats to get into my yard.

"What is that?" I ask, pointing at the tent.

His head tilts, and he gives me that boyish

smile of his. "That's a tent, Dimples. What part of the northeast did you come from that they don't have tents?"

I glare at him. "Not what I meant. Why is it in my yard?"

"I have to sleep somewhere," is his response. He's closed the distance between us. "I brought breakfast." He holds up the bag.

"You intend to bribe me with baked goods?"

"Not bribing, Dimples. Just sweetening you up a little." He holds out the cardboard cup holder. "Now then, I got two different lattes, one with caffeine and one without. This one is an iced peach tea, and this one is an iced chai tea. What's your poison, baby?"

"You didn't answer my question about the tent. And you really need to move your truck. My neighbor over there gets cranky about people parking in front of her house." I cross my arms over my chest, feeling rather smug about ruining his plans.

"Your neighbor, Mrs. Donnelly, is a sweet little thing, and once I explained the situation, she readily agreed to let me park there. I even sweetened the deal by offering to mow her yard."

You ever have those moments where you

kinda feel like smoke might be coming out of your ears? I'm just asking for a friend.

"What are you doing, Evan? You can't just pitch a tent in my front yard."

"Did you pick a drink? I'm partial to the peach tea myself."

"Caffeine," I say. "Hand it over. Evidently I'm going to need it today." I take the coffee and go to sit on my porch.

"I could put the tent away if you'd let me move in with you," he says.

"Are you insane? We don't even know each other." Even saying the words myself feels false. But I know that's just hormones talking. My body knows him, and his nearness is clouding my judgment. "I'm going to need you to stand downwind from me," I blurt.

"Is something on me making you nauseous? I didn't put on cologne or anything. Maybe it's my shampoo or deodorant."

"No, you just smell really amazing, and it makes me want to do things I know I shouldn't."

That makes him smile, which in turn makes me wet. Awesome.

"So is that a no to me moving in?" he asks.

"Yes. No. It's a no, yes, it's a no. You cannot move in," I say.

"Then the tent stays. You need time, and I respect that. I'm gonna give you time. But I'm also gonna be nearby in case you need anything because you can't keep me from taking care of my girls."

"I am not your girl, I am a woman."

"Well then, I'm going to stay close to take care of my girl." Somehow this grin is even sexier. "And my woman."

Danger, Will Robinson! Abort mission. Run away! Do not look directly at the very handsome man.

I cannot let myself fall any more for him than I already have. He's duty-bound to take care of me and the baby. So he's not even in this for me. I need to remember that, lest I get my heart broken beyond repair.

"You're ridiculous," I say.

"Ridiculously happy I found you again."

"You can't camp here."

"Dimples, I was an Army Ranger. I can camp anywhere."

"No, you can't camp here," I point to my yard, "because I have an HOA."

"Nah... I got that sorted out. As it turns out, Mrs. Donnelly is the president of the HOA, and she understood our delicate situation. She approved my staying here for the time being."

Just then, the topic of conversation steps out onto her front porch and waves at us.

Just like that he's in my life and winning over neighbors I haven't even officially met yet.

"Ugh," I groan. Then I turn to head back inside. I think for a moment, then turn around to face him. I grab the bakery bag and then disappear inside my house.

I cannot have that man. And it will do me no good to play house with him, pretending I can.

He's too hot, young, and charming. He could literally have any woman. There's no possible way he really wants me.

chapter thirteen

EVAN

I lay in the yard with my hands folded under my head. I'm not in my tent yet because there's a nice breeze tonight and I can see a smattering of stars in the sky.

And I'm close to my girls. I'm here if they need me. I can't wait until I can call Marley mine officially. But like Liam said, I need to be patient. I need to wait and give her time. I can be greedy with her once she acknowledges that we belong together.

I'm just so fucking thankful that I found her again.

I stare at the windows on her second story

that I'm guessing are her bedroom. She let me in a couple of times earlier today so I could use her bathroom. But I stayed downstairs, and she didn't offer to give me a tour.

My dick starts to harden just thinking about my sweet Marley lying in her bed. I got a peek at her pajamas this morning when she came outside. Shorts that gave me a complete view of her sexy legs. Her shirt had been sleeveless and cropped, leaving a swath of the soft, fair skin on her stomach. It hadn't been intentionally sexy. It was just her. Sweet, no-nonsense, and unexpectedly feminine and soft.

Maybe she didn't stay in those little jammies when she'd gone inside. Maybe she left them on her bedroom floor with her panties, and she slipped between her sheets, naked and bare and gorgeous.

Fuck. Now I'm fully hard. I squeeze my dick over my shorts. I won't jerk myself off out here in her front yard. But goddamn, I want her.

A light flips on in one of the upstairs windows. She's probably getting up to go to the bathroom. I've been reading a ton about pregnancy since I found out, and evidently, it's very common for women to pee a lot while pregnant.

I watch, waiting for the light to go back off, but it doesn't. Instead, another one comes on. I sit up, staring at the windows. A shadow crosses past the windows, then back again.

I grab my phone and shoot her a text.

ME: What do you need? If you're craving something, I can go out and get you pickles. Ice cream?

Much to my surprise, my phone rings.

"Hello," I say.

"You know it's creepy to watch people in the middle of the night, right?" she asks, but her voice is gentle and teasing.

Her calling me means she wants to talk to me, right? I can't help but smile. "It's not like I brought my night vision thermal goggles with me. I just saw the light go on and figured you might need a snack. Or maybe a back rub."

"Wait, you have night vision goggles?"

"Irrelevant."

She makes a chuffing noise. "How did you know I was getting a pickle?"

I'm grinning like a damned idiot by now. I chuckle. "Just a guess. Don't all pregnant women crave pickles? Something about the sodium, maybe?"

"I don't know," she says. "I always crave pickles. Pregnant or not."

"Maybe I should call you Pickles instead of Dimples."

"Do it and I will actually cut out your tongue..."

"Whoa, such violence. I don't think you would cut out my tongue. If I remember correctly, you are a fan of my tongue and what it can do."

She sucks in a breath.

"Yeah, you remember, don't you, Marley? Remember that night and how we were together. Fucking magic."

"It was really good," she says, her voice husky, and maybe it's my imagination, but it sounds full of need.

"So are you craving anything?" I ask.

I half expect her to hang up on me, but instead, I hear shuffling around.

"Everything okay?" I ask.

"Damn you and your sexy voice and sexy

face," she says. "Can you talk to me while I use my vibrator?"

My mouth goes dry. "Goddamn it, Dimples. Yeah, I'll talk to you. Is that kitty of yours needy and wet?"

"Yes. So wet."

I hear the quiet whir of a motor in the background, and she swallows a little moan.

"That's it, let me hear you. Let me hear how good that little toy makes you feel."

"Oh yes," she groans.

"I'm so fucking hard right now, Marley. You have no idea how badly I want you. How badly I've wanted you every night since that first night with you."

She cries out, and I swear I hear my name. Then it's just labored breathing.

"Feel a little better?" I ask.

"No. I need more. I left the front door unlocked so you could use the bathroom if you needed. Come upstairs. I need you, Evan."

"Those are the best four words I've ever heard. And I'm on my way." I have no way of knowing how much of her she's going to let me have, but whatever it is will be enough. At least for tonight. I leave my shoes on her porch and take the stairs two at a time.

She's standing in her bedroom, completely bared to me.

I growl in response. "You look good enough to fucking eat. Is that what you want?"

She shakes her head. "Later. I want to know if you want to fuck me?"

Her voice cuts through the tension like a match to gasoline. My gaze drops, eating up all the pale skin she's displaying. She's voluptuous and thick in a way that makes my mouth water. I swipe my tongue over my lower lip and nod. "I want to fuck you more than anything."

"Then take me. Make me feel good, Evan, the way only you can."

I think she's admitting something with those words, but I don't inquire further. It's just further confirmation that we are meant for one another.

I cradle her face, and my mouth finds hers in a greedy kiss, all tongue and heat and claiming. I continue kissing her as I cup her breasts, thumbs flicking her nipples until she gasps.

"They're so sensitive now. Since the baby. Sensitive and bigger."

"Fucking gorgeous," I murmur before leaning forward and licking at the hardened tips.

Her little noises of pleasure are giving me life at the moment, and I feel like I've never had a more important job than to take care of this woman and her needs.

She's smooth and warm everywhere I touch, and the scent of her skin and her arousal fills my nose. I drop to my knees right there in her bedroom. My thumb continues the soft brushing over her nipples.

"But you said," she starts to argue, but then my tongue is on her clit. "Oh fuck," she cries out.

I lift one of her legs and set it on my shoulder, opening her up to me. I eat her like she's my last goddamn meal. Slow, deliberate circles on her clit with my tongue, and soon she's bucking against my face. So, I slide two fingers inside. She's actually dripping into my palm, and I nearly come right then and there.

"So good, it's so good. Evan!"

The sound of my name on her lips, shouted in pleasure, makes me feel ten feet tall. She's close. Her legs are shaking and her movements against me are intensifying.

"Shit! I'm gonna come," she cries out. Her

body pulses around my fingers, and she tries to pull back, gasping, "I can't."

But I don't stop. I want her in pieces. I want to be able to put her back together with my love as the glue.

Love.

You know, I thought it would be scary falling in love. The real stuff, not the fleeting moments from youth. But the know it to the bottom of your soul kind of love. Yeah, I love her. I love her and our baby.

She shatters, and a gush of wet heat drips into my hand. She's chanting a chorus of my name and "oh God," and I want her like this every day for the rest of my life.

I place a kiss on her mound, then further up and press my lips to the rounded part of her belly. Our baby is in there. Safe and protected inside her mother.

Her fingers thread through my hair and she grips it. "I need you inside me," she says.

I nod, then pause. "I don't have condoms with me."

She shakes her head. "Doesn't matter. You can't get me any more pregnant than I already am."

"I suppose that's true. Will you ride me?"

"Yes, just hurry. I feel like I'll die if you don't fill me up soon."

I don't make my girl wait any longer. I quickly strip out of my clothes and then lie down in the center of her bed. It's just a queen-sized bed, so my feet dangle off the end, but we can buy a bigger bed later.

Her gaze eats up my nakedness, and the hunger I see there only makes me harder. She climbs over me, straddling my thighs, then pauses.

With one fingertip, she taps the ink on my left side. It's my tattoo from The Mummy.

"'No harm ever came from reading a book,'" she reads. "Nice."

"I told you it was my favorite movie."

Her fingers explore the rest of my chest, tracing over my tattoos with interest and reverence. Then she spots the scar on my right shoulder, running a finger over it.

"What happened here?" she asks.

"IED. It was a bad one, the last mission for all of us. We all came home scarred to one degree or another."

She swallows. "I'm glad you came home safely."

I wish she meant that the way I want her to. Like she's my home. Someday, I promise myself.

"I can't wait any longer," she says. She leans over me, getting herself into position, and nearly hits me in the face with her tit.

That makes her laugh.

The laugh becomes a moan when I suck her nipple into my mouth. Then she straddles my hips and slides her hot, wet pussy down my dick.

"Oh fuck," I groan. "I've never gone bare before. Christ, Marley, you feel unbelievable."

I fuck up into her because I'm impatient and she feels amazing. My fingertips dig into her hips as I pound her. Our bodies slap together, sweat-slick and desperate.

"Your pussy was made just for me," I tell her. "So fucking tight."

Her head tilts back, "Yes, Evan, yes."

I slip my hand between our bodies, finding her clit. "Come for me, Dimples. Let me feel you squeeze my dick so tight."

And she does. It sets off my own climax and I shudder her name as I empty myself inside her.

chapter fourteen

MARLEY

After making me come more times than I could count last night, Evan slept in my bed. And I slept the best I have in months, maybe years. I haven't agreed to anything other than going on a date with him tonight, but it's a step.

Maybe I can put myself out there and trust that he wants me more than his need to uphold some sense of duty.

I have been an obligation before. I don't want that ever again. And I certainly don't want it for my daughter.

It's been a relatively slow day at the clinic,

which is why I let the rest of the staff go out together for lunch. So I'm sitting up front when the guy walks in. He's wearing dark sunglasses and what I think might be a leather coat, but that seems insane in the heat of the Texas summer. He's alone, and he walks straight up to the counter.

I don't miss the fact that he has no animal with him.

"Can I help you?" Maybe he's looking for Lily's side of the clinic, the big animal section.

He pulls off his shades in what feels like a practiced move. He levels his gaze on me and I'm met with thickly lashed green eyes that look oddly familiar.

"Looking for the vet. Marley something," he says.

"That's me."

He stares at me for a beat, then nods. "Older than I would have guessed, but alright." He reaches into his leather jacket and pulls out a stack of folded paper. "These are from my attorney. You can have your own read over them and submit any changes, but I think you'll find the terms are fair."

"I'm sorry. Who are you?" I ask, deliberately not reaching for the papers he's holding out.

He frowns. "You don't know who I am?"

"No. Should I?"

He releases what sounds like an annoyed chuckle. "Most people do. But I'm Abel Cartwright. I believe you know my brother."

"Oh! You must be Evan's twin. No wonder your eyes look familiar."

That seems to annoy him, but he doesn't say anything about my comparison.

I hold my hand out to him. "Well, it's nice to meet you, Abel. I'm Marley, Evan's..." but I falter because what am I to Evan? Not his girlfriend. Just his pregnant hookup.

Abel smirks. "The woman who got herself pregnant. Yeah, I'm aware. What I want to know is how you figured out he's my brother. Was it that damn article in *People* magazine from a few years ago? They were doing a special on famous people and their non-famous siblings. Our pictures were right on the same page as Ewan McGregor and his military brother."

"I'm sorry. I truly have no idea what you're talking about. How could I possibly know he was your brother if I have no idea who you are?" I say.

"I told you who I am."

"Yes, Abel Cartwright."

He shakes his head. "No, *the* Abel Cartwright."

"Well, I'm *the* Marley Olsen. What do you want?"

"You're going to continue pretending you don't recognize me?"

I just stare blankly at him. Maybe Evan was waiting to tell me that his brother is a little soft in the head. Or at the very least, extremely egotistical.

"Oh, maybe this will help." He takes a few steps back from the counter and lifts his shirt, exposing a perfectly honed abdomen and chest. It's hairless and completely scar-free.

"Do you need me to call someone for you?" I ask him.

"Lady, come on! I've been on the cover of Men's Health Magazine three times. I've been in fifteen major blockbuster movies, two of which are among the highest-grossing films of all time."

"Congratulations," I say.

"For fuck's sake," he mutters. "Look, I don't

know what kind of scheme you're cooking up, but I'm here to make sure my brother is safe from your clutches."

"My clutches?"

"Exactly." He taps the stack of papers on the countertop. "Thus these."

"Which are?"

"Contracts protecting my brother."

"From my clutches?" I repeat.

"Exactly."

"We could make this really simple, though, and I can just pay you a lump sum to disappear from his life," Abel says.

"Oh, now that's interesting," I say. I'm simultaneously amused by this situation and indignant on Evan's behalf. It's one thing for this man to think so poorly of me, a woman he does not know, but to believe your brother is too stupid to take care of himself. Has he even met Evan, because he's the most capable man I've ever met?

Just yesterday, he cleaned out all of the window boxes of the plant carcasses I killed. He assured me he'd plant new things that would be a little heartier, but it would have to wait for spring. This time of year in Texas is far too hot to plant new things.

It suddenly occurs to me that in that moment, Evan had been telling me something. Making a promise that initially had gone unnoticed. He was going to be here, beside me, past the rest of summer, fall, winter, and into spring.

More than anything else he said to me, those words, that simple promise about flowers, reveal the depth of his sincerity. Of his steadfastness.

"How much?" I ask his brother, just for entertainment purposes.

"One million," he says.

I half expect him to put his pinkie finger up against his lips. I try not to snicker when I say, "Oh, I'm sure a big star such as you can do better than that."

"Five million. My final offer. Five million to stay away from my brother, and you have to sign a contract agreeing to never ask him for future financial resources for the kid."

"What in the actual fuck is going on here?" Evan's voice comes from the door. He gives me a gentle look. "Hey, Dimples. Can you excuse me and my rat bastard of a brother for a few? I believe I need to teach him some lessons."

"Oh, could you do it here? I'd rather not go

outside in this heat, and I really want to watch this," I say.

"Evan, calm down," Abel says while holding his hands up as if that one movement reveals the purity of his motives. "I did this for your own good."

"I don't even know what the fuck you did," Evan says, his tone thick with anger. "Except offer my girl money to leave me alone." He takes more steps to close the distance between him and his brother. "Brother or not—twin or not—what the fuck gives you the right to make an offer on my behalf? Do you have any idea what I would have done to you on the odd chance she agreed to your asinine offer?"

Abel takes a step backward.

"I would have murdered you. In the special way they only teach Army medics in special forces. No one would be able to identify your body when I was done."

"Calm the fuck down, Evan. I am just trying to protect you."

"From what?" He points at me. "The woman I love and the baby we created together?"

My eyes cloud with tears as his words hit

home. Does he love me? Truly? Can it happen that fast?

You already love him, a voice reminds me. I come out from around the counter so I can get closer to him. To Evan. My baby's father, and the man I'm in love with. It feels so right to acknowledge that, I kinda want to run outside and scream it at the top of my lungs. Except for the fact that it feels like the surface of the sun out there.

"Is that what you're doing?" Evan continues. "She is not Cassandra. Not every woman is Cassandra. In fact, if you'd get out of Hollywood more often. Maybe talk to some people who don't know what the fuck a colonic is, you might realize that most of us are decent, hard-working people."

"There are plenty of decent people in Hollywood," Abel says.

Evan scoffs.

I take the opportunity to grab his hand. "Do you really love me?" I ask.

He turns to face me and his entire demeanor changes. Gone is the hard-edged anger that lined his features a moment ago. Now, when he looks at me, his expression is full of tender affection.

"Yeah, Dimples, I'm nuts about you. Us finding each other was just confirmation to me that we belong together. I had already called a private investigator to see if I could find you. I know that probably makes me sound like a stalker, but I can't help it. I need you in my life."

"You're not worried I was going to accept your brother's money?" I ask.

"Marley," Evan says. "Of course not. Maybe we haven't known each other very long, and I know there are a million things I have yet to learn about you. But I know you." He taps on my chest. "I know your heart. You would never have agreed to such an offer. You're so much better than that." The last sentence he grounds out and shoots a death glare at his brother.

He pulls me into his arms, and I breathe in the scent of him. "I love you, too," I say. "I'm scared, but I do love you."

"I will slay every dragon you face. The only thing I'm afraid of is living this life without you."

And then he kisses me.

chapter

fifteen

EVAN

After giving my brother the ass kicking he deserved, I left him with a line of admirers waiting for his autograph and a selfie. Okay, I didn't actually give him a beat down, I just tweaked his nipple really hard. It's how he always got me to relent to things when we were little.

Then I convinced Marley to take the rest of the afternoon off with her staff understanding they could only call her in an extreme emergency. She's left me waiting on her couch while she went upstairs to change out of her scrubs.

She loves me. And even more than that, she

accepts that I love her. On the drive here, she told me about growing up without a dad. Her mom had done her best, but struggled with depression. Didn't sound like she'd been the kind of mom Marley had wanted or needed. I reminded her that we all have pasts. We all have hurts and wounds from childhood and anything else we've endured over the years.

All of those battles just prepare us for something ahead. Maybe it's something we'll experience ourselves, or maybe it's just something we can walk through with a friend. But nothing from our past dictates our future. Nothing is ever so set in stone that we can't take a risk.

I'm betting it all on a future with Marley. I know we'll withstand everything life throws at us. And we'll only love deeper and be stronger when we come out on the other side.

A mew gets my attention, and I look down to see three sets of feline eyeballs staring at me.

"Well, hello there. She mentioned to me last night that she had three cats, but y'all were hiding. Probably the noises I made your mama make, huh? Wish I could be sorry about that, but I can't."

The fluffiest of the three mews back at me,

then jumps directly into my lap. She spins in two circles, then settles down. Her purr is loud when it starts, and it makes me laugh. "Guess you don't mind me too much?" I stroke the soft fur on the cat's back. The purring only intensifies.

"Are you kidding me right now?" Marley says from the base of the staircase.

"What?" I ask.

"Ambrosia?" she calls.

"I'm assuming this is Ambrosia?" I point to the creature curled up on my lap.

"Yes. The traitor. She doesn't like anyone. She barely tolerates me." Marley sits on the couch next to me, and immediately, the other two are clamoring for spots on her lap.

Ambrosia starts purring again.

I stroke the cat and give my girl a naughty grin. "Clearly Ambrosia knows how good I am with kitties."

Marley sucks in a breath, then attempts to cover the ears of the cats in her lap. "You can't dirty talk in front of the babies."

"Is that a rule?" I ask.

"Well, maybe not a hard and fast rule."

"Hard and fast, huh? Are you putting in an order for later?"

She laughs. "You are ridiculous."

"Ridiculously in love with you," I say.

She leans over and gives me a kiss. "I love you too and I'm so damn happy right now."

"But?" I ask.

"But, I guess I'm just waiting for the other shoe to fall. You seem way too good to be true."

"Okay, first of all, there is no other shoe. Nothing is dropping. Except me on my knees later." I waggle my eyebrows at her. "But I am not too good to be true. Have you seen the ass hat that is my brother?"

That makes her laugh.

I catch her face and tilt her to look at me. "I am not going anywhere. I will catch any and all shoes and put them away accordingly. You are the love of my life and I am so ready to be an old married dude with a pregnant wife."

"Is that a proposal?" she asks.

"Dimples, if you remember correctly, I proposed the night we met."

She smiles. "You did, didn't you?"

I nod. "And you never answered."

"Maybe I have to think about it."

"Do you?"

She shakes her head. "I already know my

answer. Yes, I'll marry you, Evan Cartwright. But I reserve the right to kick your ass hat of a brother in the shin."

"You can do it every year on our anniversary if you want."

"I love you."

"And I love you."

epilogue

EVAN

a few months later...

The guys and I are all gathered at the VFW Hall for one of our weekly meeting, though this is the second one we've had this week. It's hurricane season so we're taking in dogs from shelters that had to be evacuated.

In emergency situations like this, it's all hands on deck. Beau isn't here yet.

Dane starts the meeting anyways.

"Romeo, you good with driving over to get

some of them," Dane asks. "I know our van can only hold six, but there's a smaller shelter close to Beaumont that has fewer resources. So they were looking for people to come and pick up their dogs."

"Yeah, I got it, brother. I just need to go pick the van up from Jude's shop," Romeo says.

Dane taps something on his tablet.

Then Beau comes in, his and Daisy's month-old baby girl strapped to his chest in some contraption. I don't know if Marley and I registered for one of those. Beau wears Bella a lot to give Daisy some alone time since she's breast-feeding.

This way she can pump and Beau can feed the baby with bottles and Daisy can have some baby-free time.

Despite that, it just seems practical. I stand.

"I wanna try that," I say walking towards Beau.

He frowns. "Try what?"

"Can I just borrow that?" I ask again.

"What?" He looks down at his chest. "Can you borrow my daughter?"

"No. That." I waggle my fingers towards the

fabric criss-crossing Beau's chest. "Thing. What's that called?"

"A baby," Beau speaks slowly as if I'm an idiot.

I blow out a breath. "No, dumbass. The thing you're carrying your baby in."

"It's a baby carrier."

"Are you just intentionally trying to be an asshole?" I ask.

"Pretty sure it's you who's been the grumpy asshole lately," Liam says.

"Probably because Marley is getting close to her due date and he's not getting any," Beau says.

"Can you not talk about my fucking wife like that?" I ask.

"Whoa, everyone take a breath," Dane says. "Evan, you have been grumpier than usual. It's not like you at all and you either need to let us help you with whatever is bothering you, or you can keep your damn mouth shut because we have time sensitive work that needs done."

I stare at my friends and exhale.

Beau steps towards me, he pulls Bella out of the carrier and then hands her to me. I remember to cradle her head as I hold her against me. Her sweet little rosebud mouth makes little sucking motions.

"She's really pretty," I say, my words clogged with emotion.

"Prettiest baby girl in the world," Beau says. "Just like her mama."

It's on my tongue to ask Beau how he can be so assured with the infant. Bella isn't even his biological child. Daisy came to town already expecting and they fell in love. Beau didn't think twice about marrying Daisy and claiming Bella as his own daughter.

The man asks Jack for help and together they manage to wrap the baby carrier fabric stuff around me and Bella so now I'm holding her like Beau had been. I keep my hands on the baby though.

"How can you be so sure she's not going to fall out?" I ask.

"You tie it tight enough and she'll be secure. Plus she's right there with you. If she starts to fuss just bounce a little."

"Can we get back to the meeting now?" Dane asks, his tone more than a little impatient.

"Yes," Liam says.

Dane goes back to his list on his tablet. He

covers a few more items, but my mind is spinning on so many other thoughts and I've missed everything he's said.

"I don't even know how to be a dad," I blurt.

"I didn't know either," Beau says.

"Same," Liam says. He recently adopted his wife's son from her previous marriage. Liam and Keller are two peas in a proverbial pod and no one would ever question their bond.

Bella starts to fuss a little so I stand and bounce like Beau suggested.

"Pretty sure Dane is the only one of us who had a good father," Jack says. "You don't need to have had a good dad to be a good dad."

"Agreed," Liam says.

"My pops didn't suck too bad," Romeo says. "I mean no one would have nominated him for any parenting awards, but he was present."

My phone buzzes in my pocket and I grab it. Marley's name is on my screen with an incoming call.

"Hey Dimples, what's up?" I ask.

"I think my water broke," she says on the other end.

"What? What do you mean you think?"

"I guess I could have peed on myself, but I don't think so. This was definitely a gush."

"I'm on my way. You stay put and I'll be right there. Don't lift your bag and I already have the carseat installed in my truck." I grab my keys. "Are you breathing?"

"I'm breathing. And I'm fine. You don't have to rush."

"Of course I'm gonna rush. We're having a baby!"

I head to the door, but something grabs me from behind.

"What?" I yell.

"You can't take my daughter with you," Beau snarls. "And you sure as fuck can't drive with a baby like this."

"Oh. Sorry," I say while Beau removes the contraption from my body.

"Do you need someone to drive you?" Dane asks.

"No. I'll be good."

He nods. "Well, we'll meet y'all there. Text if you need anything."

I didn't ask why they were coming or tell them they didn't have to. We're family, me and these guys, and we show up for each other.

So it was that all of the guys and wives were in the waiting room when I got to announce that Hazel Nichole Cartwright had been born at 9:04 that night weighing eight pounds and seven ounces. The first time she cried, I saw her mama's dimples creasing my baby girl's cheeks. And I knew everything had worked out exactly as it should have.

***

I hope you loved Evan and Marley's story. Please consider **leaving me a review**.

Read the other books in the Dog Tags series:

Jack of Hearts
Fools Rush Flynn
Quid Pro Beau
Love 'em or Liam
Happily Evan After
Ready, Willing and Abel
Romero and Juliette

Grab **Redeem My Heart** if you want to see where Great Dane's Dog Sanctuary started.

Keep scrolling for an excerpt from another book from Saddle Creek, TX, **Dad Bod Cowboy**

thank you for reading!

Join my newsletter for bonus epilogues, deleted scenes and a FREE BOOK.

join me!

COME JOIN my **VIP Reader Group on Facebook** where I do sneak peeks, answer questions and keep you up to date with everyone going on in Kat Baxter land.

excerpt from dad bod cowboy

JESS

. . .

I try not to use the word perfect anymore.

After growing up in the spotlight and trying so hard to be perfect for so long, I've been trying to embrace my imperfections.

Goodness knows, I have enough of them.

So when my friend Micah told me that he'd found the perfect spot for me to film my newest music video, I almost didn't come look at it.

But now that I'm here, I have to admit it. He's right. This spot is perfect.

I'm normally not a rule-breaker, but I've got to get closer to that tree. So I climb over the fence and jump down into the pasture. I pause for a moment waiting for some giant bull or something to come running towards me, but everything is still and quiet outside. The leaves on the giant oak tree rustle softly as a chilly morning breeze floats by.

I haven't quite reached the tree when I hear the distinct sound of hooves galloping. I look across the open expanse of the hilly pasture and a rider appears at the crest of a hill.

Even from this distance, I can tell two things. One, that man is commanding. There's no other way to describe it. He's in charge and he knows it. Two, he's not a small man and the horse is enormous. But there's so much competence and skill in the display that my breath catches.

I know the moment he sees me because his head tips and the cowboy hat sitting on his head tilts slightly. Then he changes course and rides in my direction.

My heart matches the tempo of the horse's footfalls and I feel breathless as the cowboy draws near. I'm originally from Texas. By the coast, so not in this vicinity, but still, I've seen men on horses before. I've never been affected by the mere sight of it though. Seriously though, can you ride a horse with swagger? Because this man is totally doing that.

And I am here for it!

As he gets closer, I can tell a couple more things about him. He's got massive thighs. Those wranglers are stretched to the limit across his muscular legs. He's frowning—okay, really that's a dead-on scowl—and despite that, he's the most ruggedly beautiful man I've ever seen.

He pulls his horse to a stop, then slides off with a thump of both of his booted feet on the ground.

I swallow thickly and just stand there waiting for what happens next. I imagine it just how I want it. For him to stride towards me, as he's doing now, with unrelenting purpose and intention. Then he's going to back me up until I'm pressed against the uneven bark of that big oak tree.

Then he's going to kiss me.

Have I mentioned I have an active imagination? It helps with songwriting. Yeah, so my mind is going wild, and then suddenly he's standing in front of me.

He's huge. Broad shouldered, barrel-chested and just thick everywhere. His pale blue eyes take in my appearance, which in truth is not all that special this morning. And his lip curls.

"Who the hell are you and what are you doing on my land?"

Read more of **Dad Bod Cowboy**

about the author

USA Today Bestselling Author, Kat Baxter writes fast-paced, sweet & STEAMY romantic comedies. Readers have dubbed her "The Queen of Adorkable." and her books "laugh-out-loud funny," and "hot enough to melt your kindle." She lives in Texas with her family and a menagerie of animals. Kat is the pseudonym for a bestselling historical romance author.

What readers have said about Kat's books:

"Kat Baxter is my catnip!" ~ Goodreads review

"Whenever I need my sexy nerdy dirty talking romance fix, I know Kat Baxter has my back!" ~Goodreads review

"How does Kat Baxter make me fall in love with her characters in just 12 short chapters? It's coz she's a freaken magic weaver with her words!!" ~ Amazon review

“You’ll instantly fall in love.” ~Goodreads review

“Swoon. I could not get enough of this story and fell in love with both these characters!” ~Amazon review

“... the chemistry between them is instant and off the charts!” ~Amazon review

“... original, hot, and a hoot!” ~Amazon review

“DAMN it’s hot.” ~Amazon review

“... sweetness, heat and humor. By the time the story was over, my cheeks hurt from smiling so hard.” ~Amazon review

“Such a very sweet and spicy story!” ~ Goodreads

“The connection between the characters felt real, and I liked the author’s writing style.” ~ Goodreads

Made in the USA
Coppell, TX
20 January 2026